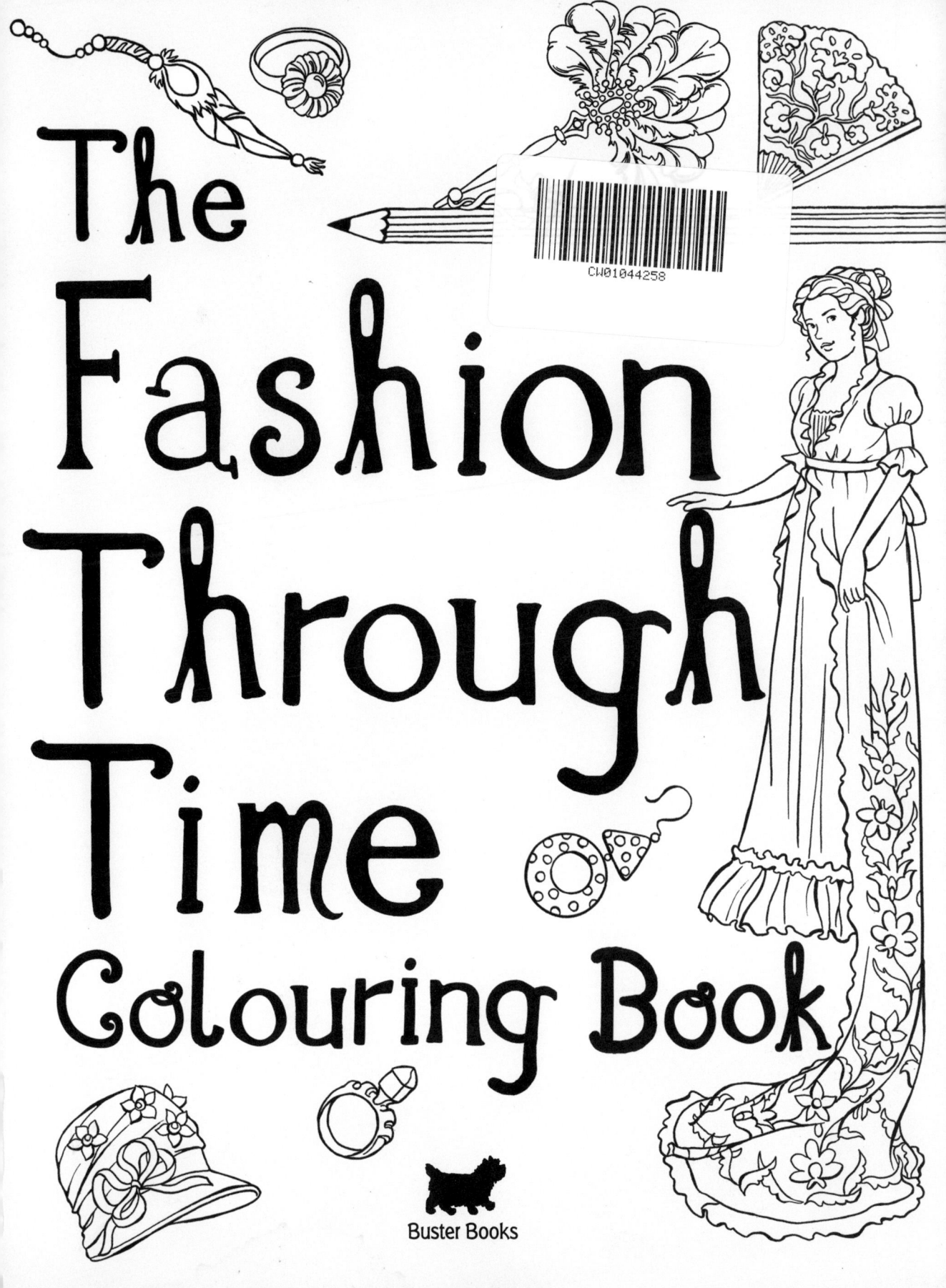

This book shows historical costumes and accessories. Some time periods are given special names, such as the 'Renaissance' in Italy. You will see some of these names in the book.

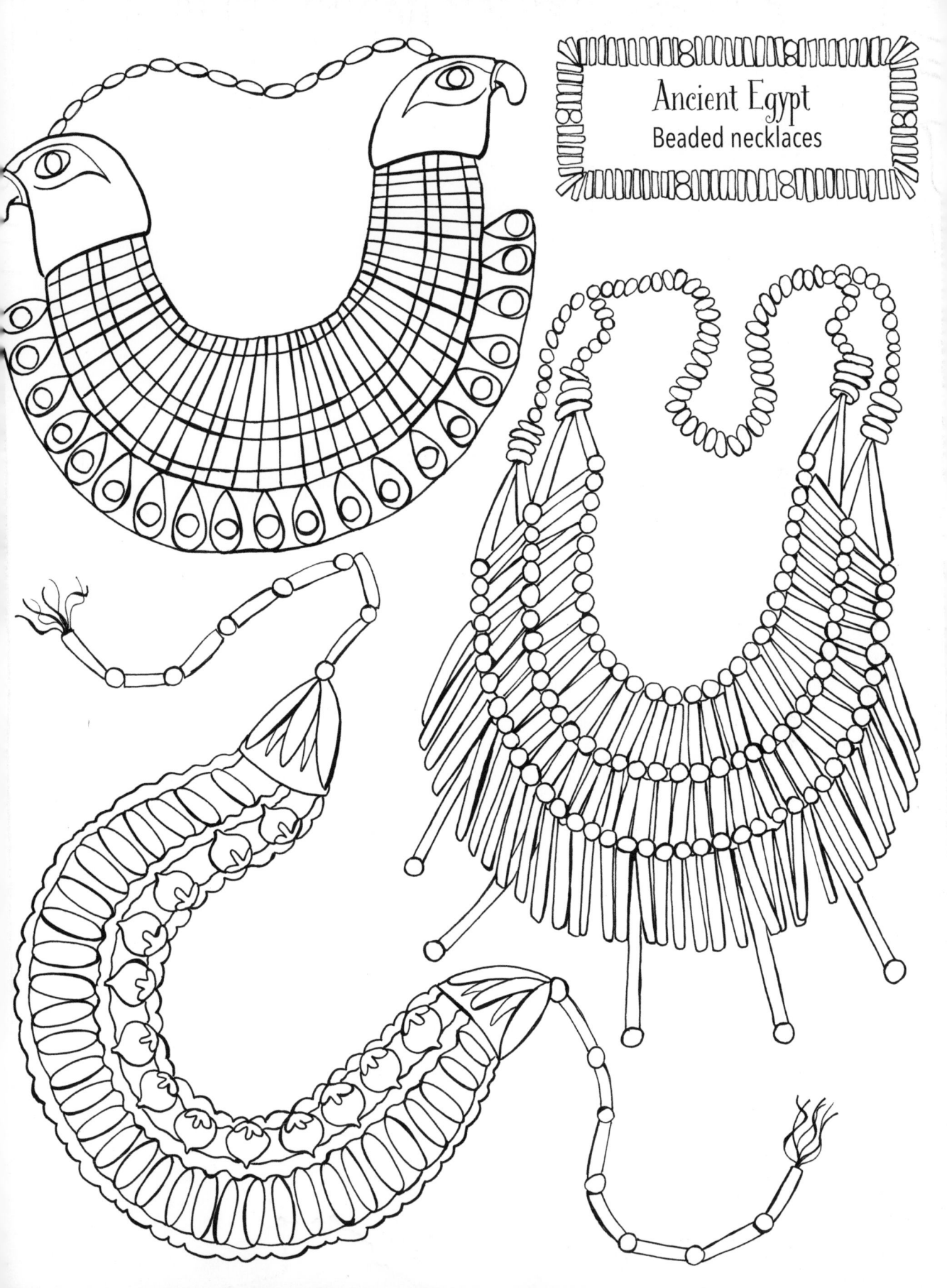

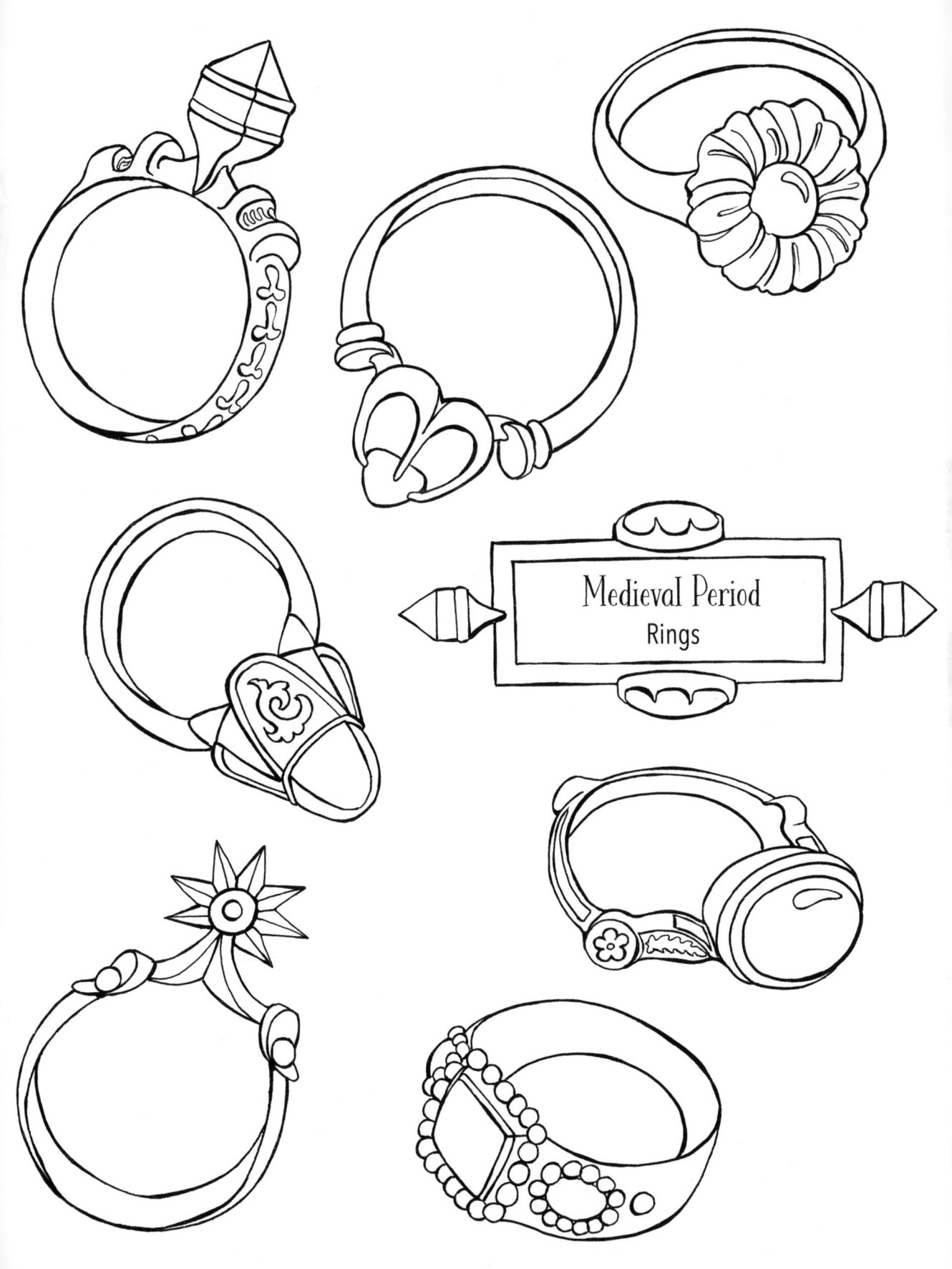

France
Renaissance, 16th century

Poland
16th century

Europe
17th century

France
Hats

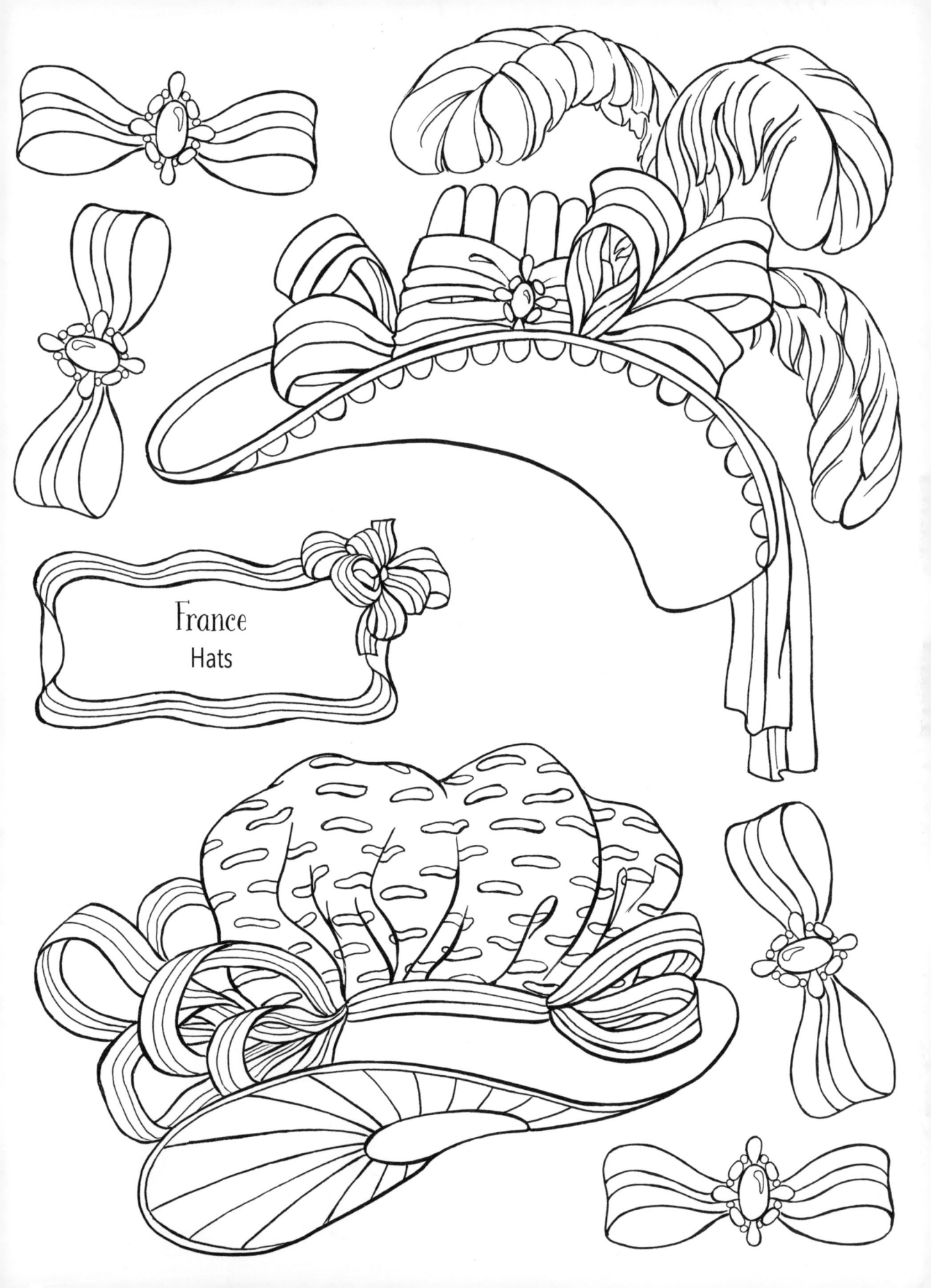

Europe
Early 19th century

Europe
Early 19th century

Japan
Edo Period, 19th century

Lapland
19th century

Scandinavia
19th century

Germany
19th century

Holland
19th century

Holland
19th century

Scotland
19th century

Scotland
Tartan scarves

Switzerland
19th century

Italy
19th century

Mexico
19th century

Spain
19th century

North America
19th century

North America
Adornments

China
19th century

Japan
19th century

India
19th century

Turkey
Ottoman Period, 19th century

England
Victorian Period, 19th century

North America
Civil War Period, 19th century

North America
19th century

Europe
1900s

Chicago, USA
1920s

New York, USA
1950s

Britain
1960s